SPELLED IN WONDER

JAELLE KEYES

Linda and Kim with Linda Edits- grammar police, plot fixers, and all-around best editor and proofreader in the world, I couldn't have done any of this without you. https://www.lindaedits.com

Get Covers- thank you for the gorgeous covers and seeing my vision. You are so talented. https://getcovers.com/

The Hangout- Vee R. Paxton, and all the rest of you – you are the best advice givers, critique partners, brainstorming helpers, and beta readers in the world. I cherish your friendships and I'm so grateful for your encouragement.

Contents

Chapter 1

Juniper

The first week of June

"Oh, my Goddess! Where have you been? I have something to show you!" Hands planted on her voluptuous hips like some avenging Valkyrie, my bestie, Blessing, yup, that's her real name, whisper-shouts as I lug the dolly holding three tubs of clothing, jewelry, and a small cooler under the canopy of our first-ever street market booth.

"Is it bigger than a breadbox?"

I grunt as I shove the acoustic guitar case swinging from my shoulder back into place, nearly tipping over as I lower the nose plate of the dolly to rest on the asphalt. Is it heavy? Yes. Is it probably too much for me to pull all over downtown instead of driving up and off-loading? Also, yes, but I'm notoriously stubborn. You should see me when I unload groceries from my car. There was no way I was willing to make more than one trip. I just don't have the patience or time for that crap.

It makes sense for Blessing to take the allotted parking space because her stuff was much heavier. Besides, her truck is big enough to carry the tables, displays, and, of course, her honey products. Three tubs are pretty minor compared to all that.

"Well, everything I found is bigger than a breadbox, but what I want to show you isn't," she answers as she tugs on a table.

I rush forward and grab the end of a table with the legs folded up as she slides it out of the bed of the truck.

"Oof!" I struggle to keep from dropping it as she effortlessly lifts her end. Blessing and I are the proverbial odd couple. She's eleven inches taller than me and built like a mythical badass shieldmaiden. She stands out, and not just because she's tall. She's also freaking drop-dead gorgeous.

I mean, if the deep red hair falling in an abundant wash of corkscrew curls down her back isn't enough to make you stop and stare, her piercing, amber-colored eyes and creamy ginger freckled skin would. Add in her gentle kindness and serene attitude about everything, and no one else can compare.

Especially not me. I'm her polar opposite. For one, I'm short, like really short. Tiny, actually, except in the boobs department. For another, my hair is stick straight and black as a crow's wing. I wear it in a stylish peek-a-boo bob, with a splash of color underneath. Right now, the color is an odd shade between blue and purple that almost matches my eyes.

Hopefully, the edginess will garner me a second glance tonight. Standing next to Blessing, I doubt it. I always feel like a little kid trying to be grown-up next to her. But that's a me problem, not her.

And then there's my mouth. It seems like no matter what I say or how I say it, someone winds up offended. It's not that I don't have a filter, it's just that I tend to be brutally honest. I don't have time for bullshit. The truth is, I'd like to be more sociable, but I suck at it. I've learned to let people see from the start what they're getting with me, rather than be left behind when I don't live up to their expectations.

My last boyfriend says I have the personality of a feral cat: cute, but no one wants to deal with it for long. He's also a liar, a thief, and a cheater. I have the court-appointed anger management classes and a lawsuit to prove it. He stole and recorded a song I wrote, claiming we wrote it together while under contract, and I tried to shove his guitar up his ass. *Asswipe.* Tamping down the anger that still hasn't abated, classes or not, I plaster a smile on my face, giving Blessing my undivided attention.

"Is it something to eat? The smell from the food trucks is killing me." I groan as we finally put the table where she wants it. "No, wait! Please tell me it's a bottomless pitcher of strawberry margaritas! Is it?"

"Not food and not margaritas, strawberry or otherwise. It's a grim..."

"Why aren't you ready for business yet? It's almost three thirty."

I look up from the task of spreading a tablecloth over the table. An older woman with bleached-blonde hair teased to within an inch of its life is standing in front of our booth. Her arms are crossed as she impatiently taps out a rhythm with one long gaudy manicured talon against a cheetah-print-clad arm while she glares at me over the rim of her zebra-striped sunglasses. Can we say overkill?

For about two seconds, I wonder if I should ask her how she wipes her butt with those nails, but common sense prevails over curiosity. I'm afraid the answer might scar me for life. There are some things that need to remain a mystery in life, and that can be one of them.

"The market doesn't open until four." I shrug and get back to setting things up. Ask rude questions. Get rude answers.

"We're still setting up, but I'm happy to help you early. What are you looking for?" Blessing smoothly takes over, soothing the Serengeti-clad Karen with a few well-chosen words. For a statuesque woman, Blessing's voice sure doesn't match her body. It's sweet and breathy, bordering on childlike. I bet she could charm the birds from the trees if she tried. She's like freaking Snow White. *Sheesh.*

See? Nice, isn't she? It's like she's the bitch whisperer or something. She seems to handle me well enough. Blessing always says, "You lure more bees with honey," which is a hoot if you ask me because that's what Blessing does. She's a freaking beekeeper and owner of Blessing's Be Apiary.

Me? I'm a seamstress. I design and sew my own line of one-off witchy indie clothing called Taken by the Wind. That's my nod to Fleetwood Mac and my personal goddess, Stevie Nicks. My stuff tends to be sexy, but with a dark rocker chick vibe. It's popular with the alternative scene, especially because no two pieces are exactly the same.

Normally, a street market wouldn't be the best place to ply my wares, but I have a pretty decent social media following. I usually blast a never-before-seen special or feature and where I'll be, and my local fans come find me. Most of the time, if it doesn't sell in person, I have a waiting list of buyers ready to snap it up the next day. *Score!*

I'm also a musician. I sing, play a mean guitar, and write songs. This is how I truly express myself. And when I have to and because I'm contractually obligated for three and a half more months, I handle the merchandising for my ex-boyfriend's band, Burning September. *Ugh.* Stupidest name ever, right? Mabon can't come soon enough.

A few musician friends and I have been practicing, and as soon as the contract is fulfilled, we'll be hunting gigs. We've even talked about entering the Battle of the Bands, a contest that's searching for new talent. The winner gets a recording contract and an all-expenses paid tour. All in good time. I have to shake off Jimmy first.

The afternoon disappears, fading quickly into evening with the steady flow of customers finally thinning along with the setting sun. As I tap my toe to the strains of music coming from the bluegrass band farther up the street, an idea for another song begins to form.

Popping open my cooler, I grab an iced tea for each of us and then get to work replacing the skirt and halter top I just sold, humming notes and a word here or there, letting it evolve at its own pace. The skirt and top happen to be the one I featured in this afternoon's media blast. It's a good chunk of change, so I'm more than pleased.

"Okay, it's slowing down. Now tell me about this thing you want to tell me."

"Oh, my Goddess! I almost forgot." Blessing dashes to the tailgate of the truck, rummages through a tote, and then hops over to me before shoving an old—and when I say old, I mean ancient—book into my hands.

Immediately, I want to drop it. It feels gritty and gross, like a chamois left to dry in the sun after washing the car. *Yuck.* The magic surrounding it is powerful, but also kind of dark and very strange. I know just from touching it, it's made from skin, probably human. I shudder at the thought.

"Gross! What the hell is that? And where did you get it?" I practically toss the thing back at her and then reach for the container of wipes to help remove the icky feeling from my fingers.

"Huh? What do you mean? I found it while I was extracting a hive from the wall of the old Iverson place." She caresses her fingers over the cover, and I shudder.

"The bees wouldn't let the crew dismantling the old house get close enough to tear it down. That's why they called me. It's a grimoire. An old one, by the look of it. But that's not the best part...It has a *bring me love* spell in it!"

I've never heard Blessing squeal before, and I'm not saying she did this time, but it was close enough that it's a sound I never want to hear coming out of her mouth again.

"Tell me you didn't!" I stare at her, snapping my mouth shut when I realize it's hanging open. What the hell is going on? Blessing is not an impulsive person. In fact, she plans everything to the nth degree. Even her backup plan has a backup plan. "Blessing?"

"I know. I know! It has the murky feel of dark magic clinging to it, but it's not entirely unpleasant, and I, of course, didn't follow the recipe exactly. I'm not casting black magic spells. I know better. I substituted ingredients. Isn't it interesting? I was hoping we could have a girls' night and could go over it together before we go any further. We could try the new session mead I made, and I'll throw in pizza..." she wheedles.

Suddenly, Blessing freezes but then shuffles backward until she tucks herself among the dresses I have hanging. It's then I realize she isn't really paying any attention to me.

Good Goddess! "We? Are you *crazy*?" This sounds like something I would do, but Blessing? She seems almost jittery and acting completely out of character. It makes me freaking nervous, and I don't like it.

"Tell me you didn't cast it already!"

"I didn't, I swear. I've only gathered and mixed a few ingredients. Nothing was sacrificed, I promise."

Oh, for Goddess's sake! This is bad, really bad. "Then what the hell is going on with you right now?"

It's like talking to a ghost, except I can still see her legs and feet. Is she hiding? From what or who? The darned book creeped me the hell out, so maybe she finally realizes how dangerous dabbling in someone else's spells can be.

"So, are you coming over?" she asks again as she peeks around an indigo-colored lace handkerchief skirt, but she's not looking at me. Instead, her attention is on the beer tent at the end of the row of booths. *Hmmm.*

"Yeah, I'll be there, but I can't do lunch or supper, how about breakfast? And I'll handle the food." Someone needs to talk some sense into her. "I totally got influenced by this hilarious Cory guy on TikTok and bought an air fryer. I've been dying to give it a test run. You'll be my guinea pig, and for once, I'll be your freaking voice of reason!" Giving up any pretense of being casual, I turn to survey the crowd mingling down the thoroughfare. "When are we doing this? Tomorrow?"

I feel the need to rein her in. Usually, it's the other way around and she's talking me off a ledge. I need a distraction, something to calm both of us down. She's freaking me the hell out. Spying my guitar case, I leap toward it and practically rip the guitar from it.

Music can't hurt, right? It is the language of the universe. Higher frequencies, positive energy, and all that woo-wooey goodness. What? I'm an elemental air witch, sue me.

Suddenly, Blessing has me by the shoulders while scrunching down behind me. She duck walks us forward until I bump into the table. Now, I'm barely five feet tall, and that's if I'm standing up straight. Did I mention Blessing is one measly inch shy of being a foot taller than me? We must look ridiculous.

"Uh...Blessing? What are you doing?" As dire as the situation seems, I can't help but giggle. Usually, it's me acting crazy. Have we entered an alternate reality where we've exchanged personalities like in that movie *Freaking Friday*? Except, I think they exchanged bodies, and it was a mother and daught...

"Oh, lickable Loki on a popsicle stick! Blessing?" Walking toward our booth is a wall of muscle and leather and worn denim and downright sexiness. *Holy shitballs! It's a bunch of bikers.*

"Shit! Don't make eye contact! Act normal!" she whisper-shouts.

"Well, there's your first mistake, expecting me to be normal," I grumble. Shrugging, I try to loosen her grip. I couldn't drag my eyes off the sexy wall of manscape coming closer and closer even if I tried.

"Oh, for crying out loud, *Juni*. I don't want him coming over here!"

Him who? "Um...too late?"

"What? Shit! Shit! Shit!" Blessing drops to her knees, slapping at the tablecloth as she scrambles beneath it.

"Uh...Blessing? What are you doing?"

"*Shut it!* Be normal!"

"Because using *me*, of all people, as a human duck blind *and you* crawling beneath the table is so-o-o normal. Ouch! You did *not* just pinch me!"

"Juniper...*swear to the Goddess*...FO-CUS...normally!"

I straighten my shoulders, holding my guitar like a shield between me and the wall of leathery goodness as they stop right in front of our booth. I'll admit, they're intimidating, but I'm made of sterner stuff. They won't be getting *me* to agree to any bargains or to do anything stupid!

"You look just like the seven dwarves, beards, long hair and all, except, you know, there's only four of you...and you guys are all freakishly tall...uh, giants, really."

You know that awkward phenomenon where you spew word diarrhea all over the place but then play it back in your mind and realize how stupid you sound? Yup, afraid so.

They stare. I stare. Thank the Goddess, the rest of them stayed on the other side of the street.

"Um...yeah. Ah...hi there, how can I help you?" I plaster what I hope is a cordial smile on my face, but from the looks I'm getting, I probably look like the Joker. The Ledger one, not Nicholson. My hair is way cooler than his. *Goddess help me, I'm rambling.* But do I zip my lip and shut up?

No. No, I do not.

"Did you know statistics show that really tall people are more prone to nose bleeds? Ouch!" I slap at the fingers pinching my thigh. I stretch the psychotic smile on my face even wider. Pulling back my foot, I let fly, delivering a sharp kick to a certain ex-bestie hiding under the *freaking* table.

"*Oof. Witch,*" Blessing whispers as she slugs me right in the same spot she pinched.

"*Umph!* Harpy," I hiss back, dropping the guitar a few inches until it bangs against her head. It makes a hollow sound. The guitar, not her head. I can't control the giggles when the instrument is yanked from my hands and disappears beneath the table.

"Ta-da! Magic!" I shout, waving empty jazz hands before me as the overly large and insanely delicious leather-clad men stare down at me. Briefly. I wonder if there's room under the table for one more.

"Hi! How can I help you?" I chirp.

Yes, chirp. It seems I've been rendered stupid by the sight of all the intimidating sexiness before me after all.

"I'm pretty sure none of my designs are going to fit you...not that I'm making assumptions about your clothing choices. Whatever floats your boat, ya know? We don't have anything here you'd want. Unless, of course, you want some honey... That I could definitely help you with. *Did I really just suggest that? And did it have to sound like I was offering up something entirely different?* I smack my palm against my forehead. "Ouch."

"You okay there, Lightning Bug?" one of them asks, amusement more than obvious if the charmingly wicked sparkle in his bright blue eyes is anything to go by. *Goddess, I hope he doesn't smile.* That would be lethal and overkill, seeing as he's the only one without a beard and he isn't quite as tall as the rest of them.

That isn't to say he isn't tall because he is. Of course, everyone is taller than me. He already has a sexy tilt to his lips that could cause a girl's panties to catch fire. I wouldn't consider him classically handsome, his features are too sharp for that, but oh, Goddess, is he sexy and somehow more appealing than the rest.

"Uh...mosquito?" I can feel the heat of embarrassment climbing from my chest, up my neck, and into my cheeks. "Hi! How can I help you?" *OUCH! Shit!* "Blessing, if you pinch me again..."

Finally, the scariest one speaks. "Yeah. You can tell Blessing, who I know is hiding under the table, to call Saint."

Chapter 2

Darius

"Yeah. You can tell Blessing, who I know is hiding under the table, to call Saint," Saint snarls at the feisty little witch.

"Saint, huh? Somehow I doubt it." She rolls her eyes. "That'll be a negative, ghost rider. It breaks the girl code. Hos before bros, chicks before dicks, sisters before misters, girls before squirrels...unless they're in the road... Oh, quit scowling. You really do remind me of dwarves. You'd definitely be the one they'd call Grumpy."

Over thousands of years of watching and serving our punishment in this world, I've seen a lot of extreme reactions to our kind, mostly fear, deference, or outright worship, at least until we became renegade bikers, but this total lack of regard? Astounding and...oddly refreshing.

The crazy woman has the audacity to plant her hands on her hips and square off with Saint, who, on a good day, is a grumpy asshole. Especially to witches.

Instead of making her look like a force to be reckoned with, the pose draws attention to her tiny waist, accentuating a lovely pair of truly generous breasts. She has a bangin' body, but I doubt this little witch could hurt a single soul.

And her voice. It's surprisingly sensual and raspy. It whispers over the skin in a sneak attack on the senses. There and gone but leaving a brush of arousal in its wake.

"Why not?" Saint grunts, leaning over the table into her space, obviously her voice doesn't have the same effect on him. As a precaution, I lay a restraining hand on his shoulder. We may be one of the most notorious motorcycle clubs in the world, but we're not dangerous to the innocent. I know he'd never hurt her, but she doesn't know that. Not that it looks like she's intimidated.

"Because then she'd be breaking rule number three of the girl code, duh." She nods like that explains everything.

"Huh?" Rake, another brother, butts in. "What's rule number three? I gotta hear this. Wait! Shouldn't we hear what one and two are first? Maybe you could explain them to me when I take you out later, darlin'?" At first, his tone is laced with sarcasm, but all too quickly, it turns suggestive as he moves closer to the table. Onyx chuckles.

I smack Rake in the stomach. "Knock it off," I warn. I swear he's a bigger asshole than Saint, just friendlier with females. We call him Rake for a reason.

"Hmm... Let me give your charming offer some thought." The witch taps her finger against her chin like she's seriously considering it. "How about no, Dopey. I wasn't born yesterday. You, Slurpy, and Bossy keep quiet while I talk to Grumpy." I snort at her names for us. She must be a little crazy; she doesn't seem intimidated by us at all.

"For the record," she continues, "rule number three is simple. A woman is never supposed to chase a man. Instead, he should be the one chasing her. He'll appreciate her more. So, if Grumpy wants a chance with Blessing, he best get his ass busy doing the chasing part."

She snatches up a business card off the table, thrusting it in Saint's direction. "Here's her card with her phone number, email, and social media on it." He doesn't take it right away, but she doesn't back down. Head tipped to the side; she raises an eyebrow while calmly waiting. He finally sighs and plucks it from her fingers.

Humph.

"Sorry, I don't speak grunting giant, but y'all have a nice evening. Blessing'll be waiting for your call. *Ouch!* Goddess, bless it. Stop with the pinching already!"

As my brothers walk away, I pick up one of the other cards sitting in a neat stack on the table. "Juniper Taylor," I read, before giving her a panty-dropping smile. "I think I'd like to get to the chasing too. My name is Darius."

"Darius, huh?"

"You gonna answer when I call, Juniper?" She's cute. Crazy, but definitely cute. Angels don't do serious, but she'll be fun for a bit.

"I guess you'll find out, won'tcha? Although, I probably wouldn't hold my breath if I were you."

Chapter 3

Juniper

Midsummer's Eve

"Hey, Blessing. How's it going?" I ask as I arrive at her side. It's surprisingly crowded. During the fair in late summer, this building holds the 4H crafts, and I've never seen this many people in it. It's a good thing. It means that although the Midsummer's Eve festival is only in its third year, it's gaining popularity. I had to stand on a bench to see over the crowd to spot her when I first arrived. "Have they started judging the meads yet?"

"Hey, Juni. No, they won't get to them for a couple of hours at least. They're finishing up the red wines right now. The rosés and sparkling wines are next and then the whites. Meads and ciders are up after that and then the craft beers. It's going to be a long day."

The whole wine-tasting thing seems pretentious as hell. Usually, this would be right up Blessing's alley, but she is seriously subdued, as if someone has thrown a veil over her sparkle. Maybe it's nerves or she's afraid to get her hopes up.

She should be excited; she's worked hard, and she's earned her spot here. It's the next step of her big plan, so why the long face? It's also the first year she's entered anything in the competition, so it would make sense. A lot is riding on the recognition she'll gain, but I can't help but think something else is weighing on her, stealing away the joy she should be experiencing.

"Feel like grabbing a bite with me before I have to get to work? The band goes on at four, so I have a couple of hours before I have to start setting up. How about a funnel cake and a fresh-squeezed lemonade?" I wheedle and then sweeten the deal when it looks like she's about to say no. "Come on, my treat."

"Okay, I guess I could eat."

"Groovy. Go grab us a spot under the dinner tent, and I'll snag us some munchies before it gets too busy."

Balancing two funnel cakes, a fist full of napkins, and two large drinks, I step out of the noonday sun and into the relative coolness of the open-sided tent. Thank the Goddess, I remembered my sunglasses. I find Blessing sitting at the end of a long plastic table in the farthest corner, staring off into space.

I set the drinks down and plop the plates loaded with funnel cakes. They are so loaded with powdered sugar they puff like mushroom clouds. Tossing the mittful of napkins down, I stare at my friend. I'm not good with the empathetic crap. That's Blessing's forte. Give me a direction or a task, though, and I'm a heat-seeking missile.

"Okay, sister, enough. Who do I need to maim, curse, or disappear?" I viciously rip off a piece of cake, then pop it into my mouth.

"No one, I guess. He already pulled the disappearing act," Blessing answers morosely.

I stop midchew. I'd been joking. *That son of a bitch!* "He what?" But I already know. Darius's friend followed her home after the market two weeks ago. He was still there the next afternoon, and let's just say there was no hiding the beard burn, love bites, or the glow of happiness spilling out of Blessing's eyes. "He hasn't called or even texted? Nothing?"

"Nothing."

"Have *you* texted him?"

"Twice." She fiddles with the straw in her lemonade before taking a drink and avoiding my gaze.

"And nothing?"

"Nope."

What the hell? Darius texted me a couple of times before he left to handle business. I'll admit, I did text him back, even if my answers were brief. At least we communicated. He let me know he was gonna be out of contact for a bit, and I let him know I probably wouldn't have even noticed just to keep him on his toes. "Maybe..."

"It's not important." She cuts me off. "Listen, I'll see you later. I gotta run to the bathroom and get back to the judging. There's a reporter from a wine magazine who wants an interview. I'll catch up with you later."

I watch her walk away, pondering the situation while finishing off my snack and the rest of hers. Hey, it's funnel cake, you'd do the same. What I do know is she must really like him. Even though she's never dated much, I can see how much she's hurting.

My watch beeps, letting me know the truck with Burning September's merchandise should be here. I clear our stuff from the table, hit the bathroom, and then make my way through the growing festival crowd, trying to decide what I can do to help or if this is one of those situations where I need to keep my mouth shut. I mean, I did already warn him she was enacting rule number three of the Girl Code, but maybe Saint isn't the problem. Maybe I need to spend more time with Blessing and go over the code again.

Tai, the drummer for Burning September and roadie for the day, is just pulling up with their trailer when I reach the mainstage area. I'll be stationed at the last booth in the row for the next ten hours or so. There are two other supporting acts who travel with Hedonist, the main act, so they get better positioning with their tables.

The groovy thing about Hedonist, besides their kick-ass music and being totally mysterious, of course, is that they remember the trials and tribulations of getting their big break, so the first band taking the stage at each of their concerts is usually local talent.

"Hey, Tai," I greet as he unlocks the trailer door, swinging it wide.

"Hey, Juniper. How goes it?" Tai is a man of few words, something I appreciate.

"Oh, you know, another day, another donut."

We take turns pulling out the things I need, and then he helps set up the canopy.

"Here's the card reader and cashbox. I'll come over and spell you after our set. Do you need anything in the meantime?"

"I'm good." I wave him off. I've turned the organization of their merch into a streamlined fine art. Besides, he's got his own crap to take care of. I don't understand why he puts up with the rest of the band. They'll usually show up just about the time he gets the equipment on stage.

He's a decent drummer and a really nice guy. Not only does he care about my welfare as the band's only employee, but he also loves interacting with their fans. After their set, he'll come and work behind the merch table and hang out.

Burning September's following loves it. I usually take a video or two of his interactions and then send them to him. Jimmy and the rest of them haven't caught on, but Tai's popularity on social media is ten times larger than any of theirs, and I take some credit for that.

Usually, working concerts and music festivals is pretty boring most of the day, with a lot of sitting around and a sale here or there until after the band takes the stage. After they play, I'm slammed for a couple of hours.

This evening is no exception, except Tai isn't the only one helping. Jimmy's decided he needs to be here too, even though he rarely helps out. If you can call it helping. The T-shirt sizes are in disarray, some of them even balled up and tossed back into the tubs where we store them. The stickers, sweatbands, and buttons are all mixed together. He tore a sweatshirt off the display when he couldn't find the right size. He's double-charged four different customers and undercharged Goddess only knows how many more, and somehow, it's my failing. With the little digs he's throwing at both Tai and me, the tension is so thick, a girl could scoop it with a spoon.

And of course, now that Tai's gone to get the truck and trailer so we can wrap things up for the night, Jimmy thinks it's the perfect time to start in on me.

Ugh. I keep my head down and pull air in through my nose with an eight-count breath, hold it for eight beats, and then blow it out through my teeth for another eight, trying to calm myself the way the court-appointed counselor taught me. With quick efficiency I reorganize the T-shirts, refolding as I go. The sooner we finish, the sooner I can get away from him.

Speaking of getting away from him, why the hell is he looming over me? He should know by now I'm not intimidated by his size. Giving him a dirty look, I bite back the scathing comment on the tip of my tongue and instead walk around the table and continue folding from the other side while loudly ignoring him.

"What the fuck do you think you're doing?" He flips his dishwater-blond hair, glaring at me from between the strands hanging in his face. I bet he practices his death stare in the mirror. I shrug and continue working.

Jimmy is a nice-looking guy, I'll give him that, tall and slim, but not skinny. He's the All-American package. Too bad his looks fail to compensate for the "I'm a dick" personality that pours out every single time he opens his mouth.

"No, seriously. You're the one throwing side-eyed looks around like confetti, Juniper. You're up to something. If you have something to say, then say it. I'm not stupid. I see what's going on between you and Tai. You're fucking him, aren't you?"

I'm pretty sure stupid is exactly what he is, because I have no idea what he's talking about. I stare at him dumbfounded and respond with the only thing that comes to mind. "Are you high?"

He plants his fists on the table between us and glares at me. "Stay away from him. He doesn't need your clingy freakiness dragging him under."

Before I have the chance to respond, the delicious scent of sandalwood and ginger teases my nose, making me shiver. And it's not because I'm chilled. In fact, it's exactly the opposite. Thick arms surround me, pulling me into the warmth of a large and strong body. My breath catches, and I still, T-shirt dangling midair from my fingertips. Jimmy and his accusations are instantly forgotten, even though he's still standing right in front of me.

"You about done here, Lightning Bug? We have an hour if you have an offering to toss into the solstice fire." Oh, I recognize the sensual voice rumbling against my ear. I've been listening to it on the phone and in my dreams. *Darius.*

To say I'm surprised he's here would be an understatement. I twist my neck to look up at him. I'm not sure if I should be angry he's getting in my business and acting so familiar or if I should be charmed he understands what's important to witchy little ol' me.

Yeah, you know which way I'm leaning. What can I say? Guys who pay attention to detail are my Achilles' heel. I'm not ashamed to admit it...much.

He doesn't pull away. Instead, he turns me so I'm facing him and bends closer until he brushes his lips once and then again against mine. He pulls back just enough that I can see the corner of his lips kick up in that sexy tilt, as if he knows what I'm thinking.

But before I can say anything, he dips back down. I hum as he captures my lips in a scorching kiss that has me rising onto my toes to deepen it. His arms tighten, but if he thinks I'm going to pull away, he's got another think coming. He might as well have shouted "I dare you!" because this kiss is a challenge, pure and simple. What he doesn't know is that I have no reverse gear. I never back down, and that's a lesson he's about to learn.

I wrap my arms around his neck, driving my fingers into his hair to grip it tight, holding him where I want him. I eat at his mouth, enjoying the most delicious tasting treat I've ever had. I'm not sure how long we kiss. It could have been forever or for just a few seconds, but I know it's the best kiss I've ever experienced.

I gasp in a breath when he finally rips his mouth away from mine. My eyes open immediately, jumping to his. *Oh.* I feel the word forming, but no sound leaves my lips, and my heart thumps a hard beat and then sinks into my stomach. He's not even looking at me. Instead, his jaw is tight, and his electric-blue eyes are intense, and laser focused behind me.

Turning to face the music, which happens to be Jimmy's judgmental ass, I realize I'm not going anywhere. I've freaking climbed Darius like a tree. My legs are wrapped around his body, ankles locked together at the small of his back, and his hands are squeezing the globes of my ass, fingers just touching the promised land. *Oh boy.*

"Uhh, hey." I shudder. *Holy shitballs!* I'm not usually into public displays of affection, but damn. This must be how felines feel. I can't decide if I want to rub my breasts all over his rock-hard chest or slap the shit out of both of us.

Darius touches his forehead against mine. "Do I get a vote?"

Shit. I said that out loud?

"You did."

I can't see it, but I know the little shit is grinning. *Gah!*

"I'm not paying you to be a whore, Juniper," Jimmy snarls.

Asshole. "You're not paying me at all, Jimmy. The band does. Besides, I work on commission, not by the hour," I retort and then sigh. "Put me down, big guy. Duty calls." I unhook my ankles, allowing Darius to set my feet back on the ground.

"No worries, Juni. You're sprung. I'll take it from here. Enjoy the rest of your night," Tai calls. I didn't even know he'd returned. Oops.

"Are you sure, Tai? I don't mind."

"Yup. We made a killing tonight. You did good. Go have some fun." Tai waggles his eyebrows up and down.

"Thanks!" I hurry behind the table, whipping the band T off over my head and quickly swapping it for the colorful crocheted tunic in my tote bag. What? The black utilitarian bra I'm wearing covers more than a bikini top would. Besides, boobs are boobs. Some are bigger, some smaller, but if you've seen one pair, you've seen them all. Still, when I turn, all three guys are looking at me with varying degrees of heat. I roll my eyes. *Sheesh.* Perverts.

"See you guys later," I call out as I stop next to Darius. He lifts my hand, tucking it into the crook of his elbow, offering to escort me like I'm some kind of genteel lady. Once again, I'm torn, wondering if I should be pissed at his proprietary manner or charmed by it.

Finally, I decide to just go with it as we wander over the grounds toward the fires that are burning low since it's getting close to midnight. One-handed, I dig through my tote until I find a small cloth pouch with the four corners tied together.

Every witch's offering is personal. Mine has elements of everything I love and what makes me, well...me. A leftover piece of pretty fabric saved from one of my designs holds everything else, including my favorite guitar pick, a ten-dollar bill, a small piece of pine snipped from the tree in my backyard, a few nuts and raisins, dried sage, rosemary, thyme, and peppermint, a spoonful of brown sugar, and, last but not least, a note of thanksgiving and wishes for a season of abundance and goodwill.

Darius remains quiet and steadfast as I contemplate my blessings and give thanks to the universe. After I toss it into the fire, a single flame shoots up as if pulled from the coals. Sparks dance for a moment within the smoke. The smell of herbs and sweet burning sugar swirls around our heads, and I know my offering has been accepted.

"That was nice. Smelled nice too. I could feel your intent within the magic."

I nod, suddenly weary, but not in an exhausted way, more like an easy languor or a pleasant lassitude. Could contentment be the word I'm searching for?

"Tired?" He must be a mind reader.

"Mm-hmm."

"Let's go, then. I'd like to follow you home. Maybe talk my way in through your doorway with the promise of a foot massage." From what I can see in the darkness, his little-boy grin is adorable and working. I'm suddenly nervous and excited as we weave our way among some of the oldest oaks in the county on our way to the parking area.

"A foot massage, huh? Well, entry can certainly be bought with promised foot massages. This is me." I point to the silver Chevy Impala. "Where are you parked?"

Instead of answering, he cups my jaw and tips my chin, capturing my mouth with his, and, like the sparks from the solstice fire, I leap at the chance to kiss him again. And then I'm weightless, until my bottom lands on the cool hood of my car.

Eeep!

I'm wrenched away from the kiss, but immediately dismiss the chill on the back of my thighs, as he smoothly eases his hips between my knees. I draw him into me until denim grinds against denim. Letting go of control, I tug at his T-shirt, eager to feel the heat of bare skin, eager for more and more and more.

Witches aren't shy with their bodies as a rule, and I want him. Naked. Now. I arch my back, pressing my breasts into him. He groans, snagging his fingers in the crochet work of my tunic as he squeezes my breast.

A wild little sound leaves my mouth as I capture his bottom lip with my teeth and bite down. Not enough to draw blood, not yet at least, but enough to give him a taste of painful pleasure. His hands continue to roam over my breasts and shoulders as he grinds his cock against my center.

"Close," I pant. "So close. Please."

His fingers tug at the button on my shorts. I nearly orgasm on a shockwave of pure sensation.

"Did you feel that?" Darius asks as he stops. "Juniper? Baby, did you feel that?"

"Yeah...yeah, you make the earth move. Less talk...more action, m'kay? Almost there."

"No, baby, listen. Something just happened, something magic."

"Like you-came-in-your-pants kind of magic? I promise...I won't hold it against you." *Goddess.* How is he able to form complete sentences when I'm a panting mess of need? "Seriously, Darius, I'm begging...put your hand...in my shorts. It'll only take...a second or two and I'll join you, I swear, no judgment here."

It's then that I realize the damned man is seriously flawed. First, he's laughing, and isn't that the sexiest sound I've ever heard? Secondly, he's gripping my hands, holding them so tightly, I couldn't get away if I tried. Not that I would. Being restrained...*oh, baby, yes please!* Yup, that just launches my libido to the red line every freaking time. And thirdly, he's taken away my joy...stick. As in removed his cock from the cradle of my hoo-ha!

"What the fuck? You're a daemon in disguise, aren't you?" I growl. Goddess, I ache.

"No, not a daemon, but I do have to go. I'm sorry Lightning Bug, but we're going to have to wait. That was a fuck-load of magic released. There'll be repercussions from a spell that big. Go home." He leans in and smacks a quick kiss against my lips. His aura lifts, surrounding him in a semitransparent ripple of iridescent energy resembling feathers on great wings. His body grows larger, skull and limbs elongating until he takes on an otherworldly appearance.

He's beautiful.

"Darius?" *Holy shit!* My leather-clad biker isn't a daemon after all. He's worse. He's a freaking angel. The angel of denied orgasms!

"I'll call you!" he shouts as he lopes back through the oaks toward the fairgrounds.

Angel or not, I'm gonna kill him! "Paybacks are a bitch, Darius!"

Chapter 4

Darius
Mabon (Autumnal Equinox) Eleven weeks later.

"Come for a ride with me. You can't stay mad forever." I offer my most charming smile to Juniper the moment she opens the door on her Cape Cod-style home. I've seen her here and there for short amounts of time, and we text and or talk every day, but we haven't spent any more time alone.

She's held out, keeping me at arm's length with either her jobs or with friends way longer than I expected, and honestly, I fucking love it. I'm used to women throwing themselves at me, but this stubborn little witch is a challenge.

She's also a tease.

She told me, "Paybacks are a bitch," but I didn't believe her. Instead, I laughed, thinking, "Yeah, sure," but holy hell, she's the one looking smug now.

Not too long after I left her panting and needy on the hood of her car, she sent me a text that simply read *sound up*. Thirty seconds later, she sent the video. A video of her rubbing a large flesh-colored vibrating dick over the soaked crotch of her purple panties as she came moaning my name.

I was pissed and turned on at the same time. I used that video more times than I could count to get myself off that week...until the next video arrived, featuring red panties, and then the next featuring blue, and then the next, and the next, and the next until I have a rainbow of different-colored panties invading my spank bank and my fucking dreams. Eleven weeks later, I'm more than ready to get a taste of the real thing.

Yeah, I could have taken the edge off with a random woman. Hang-arounds are always more than willing. But it seems since that night, I haven't wanted anyone but Juniper. I don't just need her; she's become my fucking obsession.

Nothing about that first night went the way I'd planned. Nothing has been resolved. Not with Juniper, who was only supposed to be a bit of fun and not with identifying who or what released that spell. The only things we do know is that it was released at the fairgrounds and it's something we've never seen before. It's not black and not white, but gray, very powerful, and we still don't know the fallout either.

"A ride, huh? Is that some sort of biker-angel euphemism?" She crosses her arms, covering her breasts, or at least her nipples. My witch is stacked.

"Nah, a ride is exactly that...until later." I waggle my eyebrows and then laugh as the little shit tries to slam the door in my face. Luckily, I'm quick and get my boot in the way so she can't shut me out. "Seriously, I just want to spend some time with you. We can celebrate your victory," I add to sweeten the pot.

Just this week, she fulfilled her merchandising contract with Burning September. She also won the court case against Jimmy. She had irrevocable proof he'd stolen one of her songs. I may have made a bargain with the judge to tip the scales of justice in her favor, but she'll never hear it from me.

"I suppose." She heaves a big sigh while rolling her eyes at me, but just as quickly begins to bounce on her toes. "I assume this is on your bike? Do you even own a four-wheeled vehicle? Where are we going? Do I need to change clothes? What about a helmet? I kinda like my pretty face the way it is."

I chuckle. "Yes, we're taking my bike. Yes, I have a truck I drive when the temperature drops below freezing. It's still warm enough that I thought we'd head to the lakeshore, take in some wind therapy, and then grab some supper."

I look over the T-shirt, worn jeans, and fuzzy socks she's wearing. "You look fine but put on some boots and make sure to bring a sweatshirt for later. It's cooling off faster in the evenings, and I don't want you to be cold. I have you covered with the helmet. I like your pretty face too," I fire back just as quickly.

She grins and I grin. The moment swells, magically stretching like the pull of warm taffy into something...more. Something that's starting to feel a whole lot like it's not just her, or just me, but an...us.

With a quick shake of her head, Juniper breaks the moment and leaves me standing in her open doorway. When she returns, I see the black boots she's wearing are perfect for riding. They're lug-soled leather combat boots laced damned near up to her knees and sexy as fuck. The jacket she holds is fitted and full of zippers. If she takes to riding, I'll see about getting her something more appropriate.

"You'll do. Let's ride."

Juniper

The turquoise waves of Lake Michigan sparkling in the sun as the wind pushes them to break against the shoreline creates a perfect spell of elemental harmony.

The roar of the engine, the hum of the tires gripping the asphalt beneath us, and the wind rushing past sets a mesmerizing rhythm, creating an exhilarating feeling of flying free. It's a sense of freedom I've only dreamed could exist.

Goddess, what am I doing? Setting myself up for serious heartache all for a pretty set of blue eyes and a killer smile, that's what.

Sex I can handle, but catching feelings for Darius will be my downfall, I just know it.

The mouthwatering abs my fingers have been practically glued to since I climbed onto Darius's motorcycle are nothing to complain about either. I mean seriously? Who has solid definition even when sitting?

Darius, that's who. Being wrapped around him all afternoon has been a sensual temptation. The magic of the man and his machine blur together, and I can feel myself losing all sense of self-preservation. Wanting him is stupid, but I can't seem to help it. The truth is I'll take him any way I can have him until he walks away. And he will walk away like everyone else always has, and I'll have only myself to blame.

Chapter 5

Juniper

Samhain (Halloween): Roughly five and a half weeks later.

"Darius…we're gonna be late," I pant as he steps into the shower behind me. He slides his hands over my boobs, pulling me back into his naked heat. "Hey! Don't get my hair wet."

"Then you shouldn't have been wearing that costume," he scolds as he trails his fingers lower. I shiver. Goddess, how does he do it? I'm still tingling from our last round of "jump me the minute he walks through the door."

I duck my head, hiding a satisfied little grin. I knew I was playing with fire by creating my own version of a cabaret angel costume with a rocker chic vibe for Halloween, but damn, his reaction is so worth it. I guess there's just something about a pair of booty shorts, a lace-up bustier, and soft angel wings that gets this man's motor running.

"Pay attention, witch." His hands settle on my hips. The next thing I know, he lifts me up and presses me against the wall of the shower.

I gasp at the temperature difference, bracing my hands against the cooler tiles. He tips my hips away from the wall, and I gasp again when he pushes his cock into me, intuitively knowing this time will be hard and fast. I clench around him as he works himself in deep. *Goddess.* We fucked less than twenty minutes ago. I'm amazed he has the stamina to go again so soon.

It's times like this I love being short. He can pick me up and move me where he wants me. It makes sex between us feel so much more intimate. Unless I'm riding him, we don't normally get that.

"Oh, fuck...Darius," I moan as he sets a pounding rhythm. His fingers dig into my hips as his groin slaps against my ass. The little bit of pain does it for me every time.

"That's it, baby, you wanna come on my dick, don'tcha?" he growls.

"Yesss! Oh, Goddess, Darius, yes."

"Fuck yeah, you do. Come! Come for me right now, June."

An inarticulate shout of pleasure rips from my lips as the orgasm quakes through me at his demand. He thrusts deep, groaning out his orgasm on the tail of my own.

"Fuck me." How am I supposed to have the energy to party tonight when all I want to do is take a nap?

"I just did." He huffs out a chuckle as he lowers me until my feet hit the bottom of the shower.

As soon as he sees I'm steady, he does a quick rinse and steps out to dry off. Me? I stand there like a sex-drugged idiot and stare until he walks out the door. Shaking my head, I finish my shower and tiredly pat myself dry.

I forgo moisturizing, and instead wrap myself in the damp towel and stumble into the bedroom, only to find him stretched out on the bed naked with his arms resting behind his head. Walking over, I drop the towel and climb onto the mattress, flopping down next to him with a dramatic yawn.

He sits up, snagging the blankets kicked to the foot of the bed from our earlier interlude. He wraps me in his arms, turning me onto my side, making him the big spoon against my back. I smile sleepily, drifting. *Lucky witch.* Not only does he fuck like a villain, but he also snuggles like a hero too.

"Move in with me," he whispers, breaking the doze I've slipped into.

"Say what, now?" My stomach falls. I'm not even sure if he said it or if I've been dreaming. He can't be serious. I've been waiting for the other shoe to drop, for him to get bored and move on...but moving in together? Never once did I think...yeah, no. What the hell?

"Move in with me...or better yet, I'll move in here with you."

"What?" I ask again, starting to panic. "Why?"

"What do you mean, why? Isn't it obvious?"

"Obvious? Uh...no? Why would you want to?" I try to sit up, but he captures my arms and rolls me until I'm pinned beneath him.

"Because I love you! For fuck's sake, Juniper, what did you think was going on here?"

"I—I don't know. I thought we were enjoying the ride until someone better came along."

"I'm not good enough for you?" Darius growls, his fingers squeezing into my wrists.

"Don't be stupid! And don't treat me like I'm the village idiot either. You're a freaking angel, Darius! I'm the one who'll never measure up. I'm an embarrassment. A trouble-maker. Over the top, outrageous, improper, uncontrollable, too much! I'm too much, Darius, and not worth the investment. Can't you see that?" I buck my hips, trying to twist away from him.

I knew this day was coming. I feel like I've been running on borrowed time, and now he knows! I tug at my hands. I don't want to see his face when he realizes I'm really not good enough. "Let me go, Darius. Let me go!"

Darius

Let her go? Is she crazy? I stare down into her face, reddened with defiance, and see the hurt and fear beneath her anger. How many times has she heard those phrases she shouted at me? How many times has she felt the pain of rejection? Of not being accepted for being who she is. Let her go? Never!

Juniper snarls, a baring of teeth and frustration. She struggles against my hold. She loves me. I'm almost positive.

"Settle down." Yeah, I know, not the smartest thing to say to a woman who's ready to rip my balls off, but damn it, I don't want to hurt her, and I don't want her running. And that's exactly what she'll do if I let her go right now.

She loves me. I just need time to help her see she's safe with me. I would tell her I love her too, but she'd never believe me in the state she's in. A plan begins to form of how I can prove to her that her heart will always be safe in my care, but first, I'm going to have to use a little trickery to keep her near me.

"When's your next break?"

"H-huh? Break?" She stops squirming beneath me. I don't make the mistake of letting her go, but I do gentle my grip on her wrists and start rubbing my thumb soothingly over her pulse.

"Yeah, when is your next break from touring?" Her band, Rebel Goddess, has been filling in as the opening act for Hedonist as they travel around the upper Midwest, when they can't find anyone else local. She has a few shows booked until the end of the year.

"Uh...we have seven shows between now and the end of the year. Our last gig is the weekend before Yule. Why?"

For now, I ignore her question. "Got any big plans for Yule?"

"No. Again, why?" She ends the question with a wary lilt.

"Let's bargain." Her brow furrows as she shoots me a squinty-eyed glare. *Smart witch.* Her lips pinch together. Juniper doesn't say anything, but after a pause, she gives a single nod of acceptance.

"Good." I raise her hands to the edges of the pillow behind her head. "Keep your hands here. If you move them, you lose the bargain." Her pupils dilate. *Hmm.* It's going to be so sweet using her desire against her.

"But—" I press my fingertip against her lips as she starts to speak.

"Shush. If you beg, you lose the bargain, understand?" Her breath catches, stalls, and then deepens. "If you orgasm without permission, you lose the bargain. Do you understand, Juniper? If you lose, then you'll be bound to me, to fulfill my every whim, for the twelve days of Yule."

She glares in defiance, but her nipples tell me a different story as they pucker, hardening into tight little points. *Ah there's the obstinance and passion I adore.* I wait silently until she relents, finally nodding acceptance.

"But, if you can resist me, if you win, Juniper, you'll set the terms of our relationship going forward. Are we in agreement? Slowly, she nods once more. "Excellent. Remember, the moment you move your hands, you beg, or you orgasm without permission, I win. Let's begin."

Chapter 6

J uniper

On the first day of Yule, my true love gave to me...

Goddess, I feel like my skin has been peeled away and all my nerves exposed. Anxiety, anticipation, fear, and shame vie for supremacy as I wait for Darius to arrive. Not only did I lose the bargain...I failed spectacularly.

He'd spent hours working my body into a fevered frenzy, expertly driving me to the brink of sensual madness. First with his hands on every part of me from forehead to the tips of my toes, and then with his mouth on all the best places in between. I was a sopping mess of neediness when I finally sank my fingers into his hair and pleaded for salvation as the best orgasm I'd ever experienced ripped through my body and psyche.

And when it was over, I ran.

Granted, I had gigs to get to, but working out of town was just an excuse I needed to put distance between us, and time to rebuild my defenses and make sense of it all. But here I am, on the first day of Yule, back and just as scared and just as confused as the day he shouted that he loves me.

The doorbell rings, and I startle. Slowly, I make my way to the door. Twisting the lock, I take a fortifying gulp of air and pull open the door.

"H-hey." I cling to the door, articulate as ever. Goddess, he looks...

"You look tired." We both speak at the same time.

I look like a wreck. My hair is limp. My skin is ashy, and my forehead has broken out. I'm wearing my ratty old period sweats because I have nothing clean left in my closet. Like a fool, I stayed away until the last minute.

"Um...come in." I swing the door farther open and beckon him in when I realize he's holding four paper grocery bags. I find my first tentative smile. One of our early arguments was over plastic bags and how I refuse to use them. I'm pleased he listened and cares enough to take my feelings on the subject into consideration.

I follow him to the kitchen, where he places the bags on the countertop. As he turns back, he looks me over. I feel like he sees every flaw, every insecurity, every broken promise either made or given, until he's staring into my ragged soul. I don't know what he sees on my face, but his fills with gentle empathy and he wraps me in his arms.

Breath hitching, I burrow into his strength and comfort.

"It's going to be okay, baby. I'm going to make us some coffee. I want you to go in the living room, put your feet up, and relax. Can you do that for me?"

I nod but hold on to him a moment more before walking to the sofa. It's not long before he follows me with two steaming cups.

"Black as a daemon's heart," he jokes as he hands me a cup. He places his own on the end table and walks back into the kitchen.

"At least he didn't say witch's," I mumble as I hold the steaming cup close to my face, taking in the dark smoky aroma of my favorite French roast.

When he returns, he's carrying one of the grocery bags. "Happy Yule." He pulls a beautifully crocheted lace afghan in a lovely shade of cornflower out of the bag. Shaking it out, he lays it across my lap before reaching back into the bag. This time, he pulls out a white box with a signature rose-colored ribbon from my favorite bakery.

"Oh, Goddess, if those are macarons, I'll love you forever!" We both pause.

"Well, I guess you're gonna love me forever and ever, because they're not just macarons, they're your favorite." He grins.

"Blackberry?"

Placing my cup on the end table, I reach for the box as he opens it and holds it out for my inspection.

"Darius...I...thank you."

"You're welcome, but I have one more thing for you." He reaches into the bag again, only this time, he looks a little sheepish until I see he's pulled out a paperback copy of Vee

R. Paxton's latest spicy shifter novel. "Today, you are going to rest, relax, and let me care for you. You're confined to the couch unless you have to use the bathroom or want to go lie down and take a nap."

"Darius…" I sputter in disbelief. No one's ever taken care of me before. I mean, sure, my parents made sure my needs were met until I was old enough to fend for myself, but…I just don't know. "I can't just lie around. I've got things to do. Laundry… Why do you think I answered the door looking like this?"

"Nope. I'll do your laundry, and I'm making us an early supper. Your butt stays on the sofa, or there'll be consequences." He crosses his arms over his stellar chest and glares down at me.

Part of me wants to disobey just to see what the *consequences* might be, but I really am exhausted. There's always later.

"What about you? You've lost sleep too." And it's probably…no, it *is* my fault, isn't it? Not only did I run, but I also avoided most of his calls while I was gone. I did take the time to text, but not any of the random weird shit I would normally send him. Who does that to someone they care about? Yet here he is.

"Darius, I'm sorry." I feel like bawling. I set aside the cookies and the book and reach for him.

"Hey now, none of that," he soothes as he gathers me into his arms, lifting me from the sofa and then laying us both down. "Let's just take this one moment at a time, okay? I'm sorry too. Scaring you was never my intention. I know I came on strong, but just like your sassy mouth and damn-the-torpedoes attitude, I'm not going to hide how I feel. I love you, and I'm going to show it. You trust me with your body, baby. Let me use the next twelve days to show you I can be trusted with your heart too."

I don't know what to say. He's right. I'm the witch who always has a smartass comment when emotions get too intense or uncomfortable. I'm the one who pushes people away before they can hurt or disappoint me. *He sees me.* All I want to do is hang on tight and never let Darius go.

"Please say yes, Juniper."

"Yes."

"Thank fuck!"

I can't help it, I giggle. "What now?"

"After supper, we'll light the Yule log and celebrate the shifting of darkness to light, not just for the solstice, but also in our relationship. As for the rest of the day, you'll relax, and I'll coddle and take care of the woman I love."

Chapter 7

Darius

On the second day of Yule, my true love gave to me...

"Dry your hair, dress warm, put on your winter boots, and meet me at the truck, Lightning Bug. I'm gonna clear the driveway and get the truck warmed up. Oh, and there's a surprise on the bed for you. Wear it," I call to Juniper as the shower shuts off.

It took everything I had to not join her in the shower after sleeping with her in my arms all night long. But sex isn't what I have planned for today. Maybe later tonight, but not today.

"Okay!" I hear her giggle. It's a good sound with as torn up as her emotions were yesterday. I pull on my heavy coat, but don't button it, but I do yank the slouchy gray beanie out of the pocket and slip it over my head, tucking all the hair up inside. There's nothing worse than hair clinging to your beard and face from static electricity unless its frostbite. Hence the beard November through March.

I grab a shovel from the garage, making short work of clearing the two inches of snow that fell last night from the truck and short driveway. We're expecting more later in the day and into tomorrow, so I hope Juniper doesn't take much longer. Just as I have the thought, she appears.

"Watch your step! I don't want you slipping," I warn as she hurries toward me wearing the graduated color scheme of aqua, periwinkle, and cornflower of the beanie, snood, and mitten set I'd laid out on the bed for her. It looks fucking stunning against her dark hair and black coat.

"Thank you so much, I love them! Where did you even find something this gorgeous?" She smiles up at me, wonder and adoration bright in her clear gaze.

Originally, I was going with a red theme because of the holiday, but when I the saw the blanket at the crafter's market, I changed my mind. My witch is an air elemental in every way, shape, and form, and I knew the only color for her was some soft feminine shade of blue.

I'd then commissioned the woman who'd made the afghan to make the hat and mittens. The woman included the snood, not that I knew what it was until she showed me. But I was more than pleased and made her extra effort well worth it.

"Never you mind. It's a secret!" I smack a kiss on her upturned lips, open the truck door, and usher her in before she can respond. After putting the shovel away and making sure the overhead door on the garage closes, I hop in the truck and get us on the way to our destination.

"Darius! A sleigh ride, really? This is freaking perfect!" Juniper dances on her toes, twirling in a circle before rushing off toward the horses harnessed to the sleigh.

There are two other couples on the ride with us. The first is younger and pay us no attention. The second is middle-aged. The woman puckered up at Juniper's language, but the husband chuckled and now he's being glowered at by the old bitch. Poor bastard.

I ignore them both and follow my witch, who's having a conversation with the horses.

"Ready to pick out a tree?" I ask as I drop one arm around her and pet the muzzle of the nearest horse with the other hand.

"We're getting a tree too? But Darius, I don't have a stand, lights, or any decorations. I haven't put up a tree since before my parents divorced."

"Leave that to me, Lightning Bug. Your angel has this situation well in hand." I lead her back to the sleigh, help her in, and then climb in behind her. After we ride for ten minutes, the sleigh stops among the trees and the driver hands out saws.

Of course, Juniper picks the scraggliest, ugliest tree on the lot. "Are you sure this is the one you want?" I scratch my head skeptically, knocking the beanie askew.

"What? Shush! You'll hurt his feelings!" she chastises. "He's short and scrappy, just like me. I think he's perfect."

I grin. Well, when you look at it that way…" I smile the whole three minutes it takes me to get on the ground and cut the tree down. On the way back, the old woman doesn't make any attempt to keep her voice down as she ridicules Juniper's choice of trees.

Why the old bitch is worried about our tree, I don't know, but when we get back to the parking lot, the woman ringing everyone up takes matters in hand.

We got the last laugh as we drove away. The farmer's daughter, an elemental earth witch, if I'm not mistaken, heard the old bitch. With a smile on her face and a "have a happy Yule" on her lips, she sent us on our way with a free tree and a threat to charge the old woman double if she didn't stop her nasty attitude.

"It's so pretty!" Juniper exclaims later that evening as I dim the lights and then pull her into my arms.

I have to admit, once we put on the white twinkle lights, handcrafted garlands made from orange slices, dried cranberries, and cinnamon sticks, and the assorted glass bird ornaments I picked up at the craft fair, it looks pretty damned spectacular.

Chapter 8

Juniper

On the third day of Yule, my true love gave to me...

"Another eight inches?" Darius groans.

"That's what she said." This joke never gets old. I keep the smirk contained until Darius shoots me a disbelieving look, then the giggles start, drowning out the rest of the weather report.

"That's sixteen inches of snow in the last twenty-four hours. I had outdoor plans for us today," he complains glumly. If I didn't know better, I would say he's pouting. Do angels pout? The answer is yes. Yes, they do.

Hmmm. I rub my hands together in my best villain imitation. "Maybe I have something that will raise your...spirits." I wink at him.

"Oh, you do, do you?" His voice drops seductively into the raspy growl that I love. You know, the one that lets a girl know she's about to get lucky? *Yum. Yum. Yum.*

I lean into him, offering my lips like a novitiate paying tribute for the first time. Innocent and demure, but completely willing to give her god what he demands. He lowers his head, brushing his lips against mine before deepening the kiss.

Passion flares between us, and I almost forget I'm teasing him. It's crazy. I've slept in his arms the last two nights, but all we've done is sleep. Our relationship, yes, now I can admit that's what is blossoming between us, and I want to give to him equally too.

I drag my lips from his, shuddering as I watch his tongue touch against his bottom lip, searching for another taste of me. And isn't that the sexiest thing I've ever seen? *Focus, Juniper!*

Right. "Did you bring cold weather gear?" At his nod, it's my turn to give the orders to get dressed and hustle him out the door.

The snow is light and fluffy, not good snowman-making material at all, but it is perfect for snow angels and something else. I smile as I lead him, tromping through the drifts, to my neighbor's house. I can tell he's curious, but willing to let me lead as I knock on Mrs. Murphy's door.

"Juniper, dear, Merry Christmas! I figured you'd be by sometime today or tomorrow, but why don't you wait until it stops snowing to clear it? Did Frankie call you? That son of mine." She shakes her head. "Gracious sakes, I have nowhere to go, and his plane's been delayed. You didn't need to interrupt your holiday festivities for this old woman."

"Happy holidays, Mrs. Murphy. I just wanted to let you know I was here. This is my...man, Darius. I brought him over to play. He doesn't like being cooped up."

"Oh, I understand. My Franklin was exactly the same. Never sat still, God rest his soul." She gives Darius a considering look as he shakes her hand, before nodding. "Well, carry on, then. Franklin would be grouching a blue streak about me standing here without a coat on and letting all the cold air in. If you get chilled, come on inside, I'll make us some hot chocolate, and Frankie won't notice if a few of his cookies disappear." She chuckles as she waves us toward the back of the property.

"Frankie Junior is usually here, but on the rare occasion he's away on business, I keep an eye on his mom," I inform Darius as we make our way to the pole shed behind the house. Entering the code, I swing open the door and flip on the lights. They buzz and flicker the way fluorescents do before lighting up the room. I swing my arm, inviting Darius into the building, and present him with the Bobcat rigged with a snowplow. Behind that sits two shiny red snowmobiles.

"I figure you're probably missing your bike about now, yeah? How do you feel about snowdercycles?" I ask playfully, my breath turning into a white cloud between us. He yanks me into his arms, squeezing me tight and kissing me hard.

"Work first, play after?" he asks.

"You plow, I'll shovel, and then we'll race!"

Chapter 9

Darius

On the fourth day of Yule, my true love gave to me...

"Oh, my gosh! What is all this?" The gleeful wonder on Juniper's face as she sees how I've transformed her bathroom into a luxurious spa is something to behold.

Candles flicker in cut glass votives from every flat surface. A fluffy new cornflower-colored robe and a matching bath sheet are rolled and tied with white ribbons. I put them in a basket with assorted bath bombs.

I've installed a bath pillow and placed a bath tray across the tub. On it sits a champagne flute next to a bucket of ice holding one of Blessing's bottles of mead and a small charcuterie.

Bending, I turn on the water, testing the temperature until it resembles one of the blistering pools of hell. Juniper loves it hot. I stop up the drain and turn to her.

"Let me brush your hair while the tub fills?" I brush a damp fingertip over her cheekbone. Her eyelids flutter closed as a contented sigh leaves her lips. I take my time smoothing the brush, followed by my fingers, through the silky strands, while keeping an eye on the rising level of water flowing into the tub. When it reaches the proper level, I lean in and turn it off.

I hand her one of the bath bombs to unwrap, keeping the other for myself, needing something to do with my hands. We both drop the bombs into the water at the same time. The summery aroma of sweetgrass and sage lifts on the steam. That's my cue to leave before I can't. She's a temptation I have trouble resisting, but I want these twelve days to be about her needs, not my own.

"Take your time. Enjoy yourself."

"You're not going to join me?" Does she sound disappointed?

"Not this time," I choke out as I swing the door closed behind me, I lean my forehead against it and catch her sigh. I almost push back into the bathroom. But the memory of her hesitantly calling me her man stops me. I can be patient as long as she needs me to.

Chapter 10

J uniper

On the fifth day of Yule, my true love gave to me...

Snuggled into Darius's arms, I listen to the easy deep rhythm of his breathing as he sleeps. He's slowly driving me freaking insane. One day he's setting my panties on fire, and the next he's being sweet. This seesaw of emotions is the worst and best kind of torture.

For instance, today he gave me a beautiful, raised tray of potted herbs. It fits perfectly in the window over the kitchen sink. He also hung a wind chime made of stained-glass dragonflies in the same window. Guess what color they are? Yup. Cornflower and periwinkle.

He's seducing me with the things I've always wanted. Oh, not the tangible things like the gifts he gives me every day, but the intangible things my heart has always yearned for, like acceptance, belonging, and, most of all, his regard. I'm beginning to see Darius not only pays attention, but he also sees into the heart of me. So then why is he trying so hard to keep things platonic?

Maybe that's not it at all. Maybe he's waiting for me to tell him I'm ready. Maybe I need to figure out what he needs too. And then it hits me like a lightning bolt out of a clear blue sky.

He needs the same things from me as I do from him.

Holy shit! Why did I think we were so different? I've been on my own, basically alone for what amounts to a little more than a quarter of a century. Darius has been alone, except for his brothers, for thousands of years.

It's time to pull up my big-girl panties and give this man what he needs.

I smile as I drift into sleep... This is going to be fun. I wouldn't be me if I didn't tease him a bit, now would I?

Chapter 11

Darius

On the sixth day of Yule, my true love gave to me...

Something was different about Juniper. Something lighter, but also...introspective? Today's gifts hopefully will complement her mood. We've been lazing about, eating, watching movies, and talking, but until now, I've neglected the intrinsic part of her that needs to create. I'll remedy that now and again tomorrow.

"Would you like to open today's presents now or later?" It's a silly question. I've already brought them to her. But Juniper's not paying attention. She's sitting at the breakfast nook, staring sightlessly out the window. The sweet smile she turns my way makes my heart kick. Fuck, she's beautiful.

"Here. Open this one first." I set the smaller of the two on the table in front of her and watch as she carefully removes the paper to reveal the box of fancy assorted teas.

"Ooh! White ginger pear, my favorite! And apple plum? Oh, my Goddess! Maple and blackberry?" She flips the package over, reads the ingredients, and then flips it back over to look through the little cellophane window on the front. "Darius, there are cornflower petals in this. It's so pretty. Where did you find these?"

I'm fascinated by the sparkle of moisture in her eyes as she tries to blink it away. "Thank you!" She stands up, offering me her lips. Of course, I bend and kiss her. I'm not stupid. I'll put my lips on this woman whenever and wherever she'll let me.

"They all sound delicious. Which one should I try first? Will you put the kettle on? You'll have some too, won't you?"

"Only if you open your other gift," I tease, squeezing her shoulder and then I get busy filling the kettle.

This is the gift I'm the most hesitant about. At first, I was going to buy her lingerie, but then I realized a man doesn't buy lingerie for a woman with her needs in mind. He may say he's buying it for her to wear, but it's for his own pleasure. If a man really had his woman's desires in mind, he'd buy her flannel or cotton or fabrics that are comfortable no matter her mood.

"What do you think?" I ask as she folds away the layer of tissue the present is wrapped in. For being considered a crazy woman, Juniper shows extreme care when unwrapping each gift. I get the feeling no one has ever taken the time to care for her right.

"Darius...this is...wow!" She runs her fingers over the silky shiny fabric, tracing the pairs of golden cranes walking among sprays of cherry blossoms. "It's gorgeous. Thank you! There's enough fabric here to make so many things. Ideas are flooding my brain already!"

"I hope you don't mind it isn't quite in the same color scheme as most of your other gifts."

"No, I don't mind. This mulberry, pink, and gold is perfect!"

I laugh, but sigh in relief. "I'm gonna assume I won't see you for the rest of the day once you disappear into your sewing room."

"No. Today I want to play." She drops her chin, seductively peering up at me through her lashes. "You finish making the tea, and I'll be right back." She grabs the bolt of fabric, hugging it in her arms as she hurries out of the kitchen.

***

"Skip, skip, draw two, draw two more..." Juniper giggles.

"Are you serious? Come on!"

"Draw four, green, skip, wild, yellow. UNO, red, and I'm out!" She crows as she jumps from her chair, doing an obnoxious victory dance through the kitchen and into the living room.

I look at the board game sitting off to the side waiting to be played, and I have reservations. If she's kicked my ass at twelve hands of Uno, how am I gonna fare with a game where the title itself is an apology? Yeah I'm leaving that one alone. But...I could bargain with my brothers, set them up against her, and then turn her lose.

"What is that evil smile for? Are you planning revenge, loser?" Juniper goads as she leaps at me, wrapping her arms and legs around me like she's a spider monkey. My hands instantly land on her butt, supporting her, but the squeeze? Yeah, that's all for me. I'm definitely the winner here.

Chapter 12

J uniper

On the seventh day of Yule, my true love gave to me...

Fragments of words, notes, vibrations, and rhythm pours from my mouth and fingertips against strings and wood. The song that started months ago when I first rode on the back of Darius's bike emerges like a leviathan from the depths. Back then was just the beginning. They do that, songs, that is, coming back in bits and adding pieces here and there when the time is right.

Darius's gift today is some blank sheet music and a glass fountain pen and matching inkwell, and a bouquet of custom guitar picks nestled within the pretty bluish-purple blossoms of dried bachelor's buttons.

Tears welled in my eyes as I thanked him quietly, somewhat overwhelmed by the sweetness of this man's commitment to me. I fled to my music room in the basement, compelled to capture the moment in words and music.

It comes together like a spell being constructed, adding a dash of this and a spoon of that, stirring, while heat, intent, and patience combine until the ingredients I've been given are ready. All it needs is one more note, word, or moment and then the magic of it can be cast.

I yawn and try to stretch away the stiffness of sitting in one position too long. I've left Darius to his own devices for the better part of the day. Rising, I set my guitar on its stand

and blearily make my way up the stairs. Darius, of course, is there. I walk into his arms, marveling at the pleasure it brings to have someone waiting for me.

"That was beautiful. Powerful," he remarks.

"The music?" I never thought about anyone else listening to it before while creating it. The one and only time I allowed anyone else into my space, my music was stolen. With Darius, I never have to worry. I know that now. "It's not finished yet. It's still missing a piece, but it'll come to me."

"All in good time," he agrees and then changes the subject. "I made your favorite chicken gnocchi soup. Are you hungry?" Just as he asks, my stomach growls. "That's a yes. Sit down." He laughs.

"It smells divine. Let me wash up first?"

"Of course. How about dinner and a movie?"

I nod enthusiastically. "That sounds perfect. I'll set up the TV trays in the living room. Be right back."

Chapter 13

Darius

On the eighth day of Yule, my true love gave to me...

"It's occurred to me that I'm an oath breaker." I drop a shallow plastic tub on the sofa next to Juniper.

"A what, now?" She places her finger in the book she's reading to mark her place and looks at me with a furrowed brow.

"An oath breaker. I once upon a time promised you a foot massage to get me in your door but said foot massage never happened...that is until now. Stand up," I order.

Juniper jumps to her feet. I lay a towel over the floor in front of the sofa where she was sitting but realize this isn't going to work. She's too short unless she sits forward on the cushion, and that won't be comfortable unless I make some modifications. "Wait right here."

I hurry to her bedroom and the guest room and snag every pillow she has off the beds and return to her. This better be enough.

"Okay, sit down, feet flat on the floor." Once she's seated, I stuff multiple pillows behind her until she's propped up. "Comfortable?"

At her nod, I place the tub at her feet and return to the kitchen to get the rest of the supplies. After filling the tub with hot water, I add a pouch of foot spa salts. The heady aroma of eucalyptus and sweet oranges fills the space between us as it foams.

Checking the temperature, I add a bit of cold water. "Okay, time to soak." I roll the legs of her yoga pants to her knees, sliding my palms over her smooth calves. A zing of excitement hits me low in the gut, tightening my groin.

How is it that something as innocent and ordinary as revealing a woman's limbs can bring so much pleasure? Her breath catches, letting me know she feels it too. I guide her feet into the tub.

Sitting down next to her, I ask her to give me her hand. I place a dollop of lotion on it and then smooth it into her skin, making sure to palpitate each of her slim fingers before pressing my thumbs into her palms and working over the back of her hand. After the lotion is thoroughly rubbed in, I switch to the other hand. I take my time, pushing us both up the slippery slope of passion.

Strangely enough, neither of us says anything while I minister to her, but words aren't necessary. I push up off the sofa and drop to my knees. Juniper's eyelids flutter closed. Taking hand towels from the stack of supplies, I pat dry her feet, leaving them wrapped up while I remove the cooling tub of water.

I do the same massage on her feet as I did on her hands. Juniper groans as I press my thumbs into the arches of her feet using a strong pressure. It's a raspy, sexy noise that sets my blood on fire.

My gaze jumps to her face. Her eyes are still closed, but she's squeezing them tightly and she's sunk her teeth into her lower lip.

I move my hands up, wrapping my fingers around her calves just above her ankles. With a firm grip, I move her limbs outward as I surge upward into her space. I keep my hands moving to her knees, over her supple thighs, until I reach her waist.

"Lift," I order. Juniper arches her back against the pillows, knowing exactly what I need. When she's raised her ass high enough, I peel the yoga pants away, revealing her neatly trimmed mound. I like that she doesn't wax. I want a woman, not a prepubescent little girl. I may be a dominant bastard, but I'm nobody's daddy.

I pull until her hips are just off the edge of the sofa and her legs drape over my shoulders. It takes a moment to adjust the pillows beneath her so she's supported, but also the perfect height for worshiping.

She's spread open, vulnerable to my gaze, to my touch, but Juniper holds all the power. It's a sublime gift when a woman places herself in your hands. It creates a transcendence that can only be honored properly.

Her heady scent is an aphrodisiac to my senses. Wetness glistens on her soft lips, offering proof of her arousal. It beckons me to taste, to get my mouth on her. To gorge myself on the sweetness so willingly offered.

Some men don't like going down on a woman, but me? I love it. I'm more than happy to satiate myself on Juniper's pussy whenever I can. I crave her like a thirsty man clawing and dragging his way through the desert to find life-affirming water.

Juniper hums a little sound of approval as I spread her further and set my lips against her center and lap up her juices. I work her up, nibbling at her nub while working first one finger and then another into her entrance. Pulling back, I take a moment to admire how flushed she's become before diving back in.

Bodily, I push us onto the sofa until I have her almost doubled in half. Pumping two fingers of one hand into her channel, I set a driving rhythm against the nubby patch of her G-spot. With the other hand, I squeeze a taut bare cheek as slick moisture runs down the crack of her ass. Capturing some on my thumb, I stroke it over her anus, once, and then again.

On a high breathy wail, Juniper's muscles clench tight and then begin spasming. Gulping in deep breaths of my own, I slow my movements, but I'm too keyed up to stop, so I caress her until she sinks her nails into my wrist, letting me know she's too sensitive.

I pull away, but only until I can find my feet. Scooping her into my arms, I head for the shower we both need.

Chapter 14

Juniper

On the ninth, tenth, eleventh, and twelfth day of Yule, my true love gave to me...

We stayed wrapped up in each other for three days, fucking like daemons until finally, we both dropped off into an exhausted slumber last night. No room in my house was off-limits. Not the kitchen, not the laundry room, and certainly not the bedrooms.

Today is the twelfth and final day of our bargain, and I'm way past being tender. I'm freaking sore!

Something has changed over the last few hours. Something immense and anticipatory is waiting for a final piece to slide into place. So, despite being worn out but content, I'm fidgety too.

"I have something for you," Darius says softly from the archway.

"No-o-o! I can't!" The protest falls somewhere between a whine and a giggle. "You broke me, Darius. My hoo-ha is temporarily out of order until further notice! And just look at my lips!" I pucker up, presenting him with my puffy reddened moue. "By the Goddess, Darius! Everyone who sees me is gonna know what we've been up to these last few days."

Despite my complaints, my damned traitorous body doesn't seem to get the message. It begins to quicken as his gaze heats and a pleased grin touches his lips. All the man has to do is crook his finger and I'd happily follow him back to the bedroom...or the table would work too.

"Good. I want everyone to know you're mine. And you are mine, aren't you, Juniper?"

Here it is. This is where I give him every part of me. Can I do it? But then I realize, yes, yes, I can, because I already did months ago. I gave him my heart the first time I climbed on his bike. My head just needed to catch up.

"Yeah, Darius. I'm yours."

"And you love me?"

"Yes, Darius. I love you."

His smile could rival the sun, but then he pauses and looks at me oddly. "I feel... Do you feel...that?"

Oh, here we go again. "What is it?" I do feel something. Alarmed, I hop from the stool and go to him when he holds out his hand to me.

"I want to try something. Do you trust me?"

"Of course, whatever you need." He's starting to worry me.

He leads me to the sink and picks up the paring knife I'd rinsed and set in the dish drainer after I'd peeled an apple. I gasp as he raises the knife and nicks my lip. As the blood begins to flow, he does the same to his own.

He then captures my mouth, combining our blood with a heated kiss. Magic swells, snapping into place. *Ah-ha!* This is what I've been waiting for. This is the missing piece. The next move. I feel like I've stepped inside a hollow cavern, or maybe it's a bell, because the ringing gong that sounds spills us both to our knees.

I become aware of the magic and that we are one vessel. There's a rending away of our old selves even as something new spills in between the uneven beats of my heart and his. Blinding pain as hot as molten lava rushes through us from him into me and back into him, pushing out all thought. My scream pushes into his mouth even as I take his into my own.

Stars and light and cosmos take shape within the emptiness swirling like mist within my mind. I watch universes grow and fade and grow again as I stand on the edge of a new precipice.

A quickening so bright and filled with golden euphoria spills over, and I'm lost. Lost to the winds of blissed-out ecstasy flowing like a river between us.

I can't say I lose consciousness, because I become consciousness, and time ceases to exist. But when I can finally reason again, Darius is whispering one word over and over, his fingers stroking lovingly over my hair and temple.

"Solara...Solara...Solara..."

"D-Darius?" Energy I've only seen once before in the form of transparent wings and feathers shimmers around us. "Darius, what's happened?"

"Juniper." He breathes my name in wonder. "The old ones have fulfilled their promise. You are my Solara—the sun at the center of my universe—and you will live forever now, immortal, by my side, and loved...always."

"Say what, now?"

The end for now...

What's next? Spelled In Magic!

DOWN TO THE BOTTOM –DOROTHY

Blessing

"Bring me another IPA and her glass of water, sweet thing." My date, Jared, orders the hostess. He's paying more attention to the rowdy crowd at the bar and the ball game playing on every third TV screen as he seats himself on the high-back stool of the pub table she's shown us to.

"Actually, I'd like a ginger ale, please." What I really want is to try one of the micro-brews, but twenty minutes into this date, which was literally the drive from my house, he insisted on picking me up at to the restaurant, and I already know I won't be drinking any alcohol.

When he called, I thought he was being a gentleman by insisting he come to my door, but now I wonder if it's because he likes to control everything or he needs a captive audience. Not that I'd stay if I wanted to leave. Yeah, I'm not that girl.

Still, what's that saying about kissing frogs to find a prince?

Jared's not bad looking. In a slick privileged way, he's maybe a step above average. He's the typical Midwestern jock type still stuck in his high school glory days. His hair is a sandy blond, and eyes are bluish gray. He's an inch or so taller than me, but he's already started to soften around his middle and chin, and I wonder how old he is. Witches tend to age well. Maybe he's older than he looks?

He may be a witch, but he's bottom of the barrel, magic-wise. Males usually are. I felt the small spell spread across my fingers when he shook my hand, probably an attraction or fertility spell given to him to use on me, if my mother is involved.

Too bad for all of them I'm an elemental witch and I live outside coven power structure. My personal protections nullified that nonsense with a fizzling pop. If it weren't for his coven's power boosting him, Jared could easily pass as a normal human.

I should probably be pissed at their high-handed trickery, but honestly I half expected it when my brother Allan begged me for a favor. I've learned to plan accordingly. My mother is who she is—controlling and power hungry—and Allan will do just about anything to please her.

Expecting them to act differently would be like trying to keep white dog fur off black pants. Impossible. I just made sure my magic and psyche were balanced and well-grounded before Jared arrived. Another perk of being an earth elemental.

I tug at the cuff of my denim jacket, searching for something nice to say as an awkward first-date lull stretches between us. We hadn't talked or texted much other than him insisting he drive me. Probably another of my mother's mechanisms to get what she wants.

"Have you..." been here before? I grimace as the cheer of the crowd and then his voice ringing out two seconds behind them cuts me off. According to my brother, Jared's parents have vacation property in the area, which in mother's mind makes us the perfect match.

Thankfully, I'm saved from another attempt by the arrival of the waitress. "Hi, y'all, here are your drinks. My name is Bethany, and I'll be your server tonight."

"Took you long enough." Jared snipes as he grabs his beer the moment she places it on the table and takes a long drink, draining half of it.

"I'm sorry, par for the course on a Friday. You're lucky you got here early. We're run ragged from open to close. Are you ready to order, then?" she chirps. Good for her; his poor manners don't seem to faze her in the least.

"Yeah, I'll have the bacon jacked craft burger, medium rare with everything, and an order of sweet potato fries. Bring the lady a garden salad with low-cal dressing. That'll be on separate checks."

Separate checks? This is our first date, so I don't mind paying for my own meal, I prefer it actually, but I'll be damned sure I'm going to order what I want to eat.

"The lady will also have the bacon jacked craft burger, done well, no tomato, please, I'm allergic. Can I get extra bacon on that?"

"You sure can!" Bethany grins wickedly. "A side comes with your burger. Do you want the salad?"

"No, thank you. I will have the salt and vinegar fries though. I've heard they're fabulous here."

"They are! All right, I'll get this in for you right away!"

I love her enthusiasm.

"Babe," Jared scolds, his disappointment clear.

Babe, really? He doesn't know me well enough to call me by anything other than my name. He isn't my daddy, and he certainly isn't my boyfriend or spouse.

"Jared?" See how respectful I am, Dickhead? I can actually use people's given names.

"I would think a girl like you would want to minimize your calorie consumption, is all. You know what I mean," he grumbles, giving me the once-over from my breasts to the top of my head.

A girl like me? If my bestie Juniper were here, he'd probably already be scrabbling through a puddle of his own tinkle looking for his teeth.

"No, no, I don't know what you mean. Why don't you spell it out for me."

"Babe."

"My name is Blessing, Jared. Please use it."

"All right, Blessing. You're a big girl." He shrugs and crosses his arms over his chest like he's imparted a vital piece of information that's going to knock my world off-kilter.

Yeah, I'll admit at one inch under six feet tall, I am a big girl. My dad and brother are tall, my mother is average in height, so it stands to reason I would be taller than most girls. I am what I am. I can't change it like I would my hair color or swapping out a skirt for a pair of pants, and I refuse to go through life slouching.

I may be tall and have lush hips, but I'm healthy. I'll admit I could use a little more padding up top to balance me out, but body image has never been one of my problems, even if it seems to be for other people.

I guess there comes a time in every woman's life where she wonders if she'd be better off alone. It's only been a half an hour, and I think I've reached that point. And not just with this date, but dating in general.

If it wasn't for my mother's constant harping about the next generation, I'd skip dating entirely. What my mother hasn't seemed to realize yet is that I'm not coven. I've never been coven, and I don't need the constructs to fuel my magic. I'm solitary. An elemental witch with ties to earth magic, and Elementals are born, not bred.

Sure, I'd like a child or two, but there is no way I would ever let my children experience the things I did. Besides, I'm only thirty. I'm still considered young and have plenty of time to find a Mr. Right. If I want one, that is. It's only by a quirk of DNA that we witches live twice as long as normal humans. And if you're bonded to another witch? The possibility of living past the age of five hundred is normal.

Jared drains his first beer and then belches. He wipes his mouth on his arm and grins.

Girl, let me tell you, when your dating choices are between slim and none? Do yourself a favor and choose none. Who wants to be tied to a uncouth dick for hundreds of years? Yeah, me neither.

"Why don't we eat, and then you can drop me back at home. We'll chock this date up to irreconcilable differences and part ways. No harm, no foul, and our mothers should be satisfied we gave it a try, right?"

He grunts and turns his attention to the row of televisions above the bar and continues to ignore me.

Almost two hours later, he's finally driving me home. Yes, the restaurant was slammed, but Jared also sent his meal back twice, both times for stupid picky reasons. I mean, who cares if the pickle used as a garnish touches your fries? They wind up in the same place anyway.

"I feel like we may have gotten off on the wrong foot. Let's stop for a drink someplace so I don't have to lie to my mother when she asks how we got along."

Ugh! No! "Mmm...we didn't. Get along, that is. I mean...we're just not suited. There isn't any reason to waste..."

"No, see, you think I'm a jerk! Give me a chance to make up for it. I let my frustration at something earlier in the day ruin our evening. Please, let me apologize properly. I insist."

He is a jerk and he cut me off again! I really, really just want this night to be over, but what do I do? I fudging cave under pressure again.

"Very well." I sigh. "But only one drink." How do I let myself get talked into these situations? I'm too nice, that's how. That and I've always had trouble telling people no. Sure, I stood up for myself earlier, but it seems I've reached my quota in the balls department today.

We ride in silence, me contemplating getting a backbone, until he pulls into the parking area for cars and trucks across the street from the Abyss, a bar and the clubhouse owned by the Fallen MC.

"Jared, what are you doing? Why are we stopping here?" I bite my lip as I glance across the road. The gates look like a huge ravenous maw. The asphalt drive snakes toward the road like a black tongue licking up the light, daring those brave or stupid enough to enter.

Several motorcycles sit off to the side of the rough-hewn roadhouse-style building sitting at the top of a slight incline like a gargoyle hunched on top of a castle wall. Glaring and watchful, ready to tear interlopers to shreds at the slightest infringement. I shiver. You just don't go traipsing into a motorcycle club's house without an invitation.

"It'll be fine. You can sit at the bar while I handle some business. Let's go." He pushes out of the car before I can respond. I watch in the side mirror as he comes into view and stops at the back of the car.

Business? What business would he have with the Fallen? Is he crazy? I sit there, unsure of what to do. I don't want to go in there, I want to go home. Dammit! If Juniper wasn't working, I'd call her for a ride, but she is, so I guess I'll have to call a rideshare. Hopefully, they'll take fares into rural areas.

I squeal as my door is yanked open. "We don't have all night. Come on," Jared demands impatiently.

"I'll wait here."

"No. I'm not leaving you in the car in a parking lot. You never know what or who could be lurking in the dark, but I'll protect you." Oily amusement slides across his face.

I snort. Like he could. It'd probably be the other way around. Creep.

He grabs my arm, hoisting me none too gently out of the car.

"Hey!" I yank my elbow away from him. The stupid jerk won't leave me in the car because it's dangerous, but yet he'll force me to walk into a tavern filled with outlaws? Unbelievable. As soon as he's not paying attention, I'm out of here, and I swear I'm done bending to my mother's matchmaking schemes. Enough is enough.

"Fine! Let's get this over with." The sooner I can be rid of him, the better. I stomp across the road, up the menacing driveway, pausing to gather some courage on the porch. Fear and irritation fuel me as the clash of loud classic rock pours out the saloon-style doors assaulting my senses.

Briefly, I wonder how they keep the mosquitos out, but then I mentally kick myself for wondering about stupid things that will hardly matter if I'm dead or Goddess only knows what else.

Shaking back my hair, I lift my chin and take a fortifying breath. I may be scared, but no one else needs to know it. I push through the swinging doors and stop to take in the tavern and let my magic adjust. Earth magic is normally a gentle magic, until it isn't. It rises, swirling around me, and then merges seamlessly with the magic of the bar. Huh. Instantly, I feel the weight of several eyes on me.

I've heard that the Abyss has a type of magic that shows all who enter what they expect to see. I'll admit, I'm a bit disappointed. To me, it looks like a normal tavern. The lights are low, with splashes of brightly colored neon along the walls. There's a dance floor and booths, pool tables and dartboards. A long dark wood bar stretches across one wall, with the backbar lit up like the Fourth of July and all the different bottles gleaming and sparkling under the lights.

Jared steps in, brushing up against me before resting his hand on my hip. Oh, hell no, Creepy McCreepster. The urge to turn around and knee him in the balls and run back out the door is almost overwhelming, but in for a penny, in for a pound, I quick-step away, breaking the contact.

"Go order a drink and try not to piss anyone else off." His voice is low and tight.

Good. If I'm not happy, he shouldn't be either. Without looking back, I flip him the bird and walk to the bar like I don't have a care in the world. The sooner he's distracted, the sooner I can scoot right back out that door.

Reaching the bar, I dig my phone out of my bag and send Juniper a text letting her know the situation and where I am if she doesn't hear from me. I know she's going to freak, so I downplay the situation, but I also want to be smart. Yeah, right, Blessing. If you were smart, you wouldn't have agreed to this in the first place. Then I take a few seconds to search the app store for a rideshare and hit the download button. When the little wheel begins spiraling, I decide I'm gonna need a drink tonight, after all. Catching the sexy bartender's attention, I order my favorite drink.

"Rum old-fashioned sweet, please."

To continue reading SPELLED IN MAGIC click here!
https://books2read.com/u/bxN7OJ

About Jaelle

Hey there,

Thank you so much for reading Spelled In Wonder!

I write the romance stories I love to read. Paranormal, contemporary, alternate realities? MF, MFM, Misfit witches, motorcycle clubs, shifters, humor, spice, and action? Anything goes as long as there's an HEA!

In reality, I'm just a quirky girl with an enormous love for reading those meant to be, happily ever after, romance stories. Give me a cup of coffee or tea, a crunchy sweet, a good love story, and maybe a fuzzy pup or two to snuggle, and I've found my happy place. Sound familiar? Then we should be friends!

Please consider joining my reader's group- **Bean Stalkers & Book Reapers** and my author page **Jaelle Keyes** on Facebook and you can find all my social media links here: https://linktr.ee/JaelleKeyesAuthor

My books are available on several platforms. You can find them, signing events I'll be attending, and stay current with new releases by subscribing to my newsletter on my website: https://www.jaellekeyes.com

I appreciate you.

Happy reading,

Jaelle